For the new
"bunny!"
Easter 1993
Mom & Dad

BUNNIES · BUNNIES · BUNNIES

A Treasury of Stories, Songs, and Poems

Compiled by Walter Retan

Illustrated by Christopher Santoro and other illustrators

Silver Press

This book is dedicated to Carolyn Ewing
for her help and inspiration.

Produced by Parachute Press, Inc.

Text copyright © 1991 by Parachute Press, Inc. Illustrations copyright © 1991 by Evelyn Johnson
Associates.

Design by Michel Design.

Published by Silver Press, a division of Silver Burdett Press, Inc.
Simon & Schuster, Inc.
Prentice Hall Bldg., Englewood Cliffs, NJ 07632
Printed in the United States of America
10 9 8 7 6 5 4 3 2 1

Library of Congress Cataloging-in-Publication Data

Bunnies, bunnies, bunnies / compiled by Walter Retan; illustrated by Christopher Santoro
and others.
    p. cm.
    Summary: A collection of stories, poems, and songs featuring rabbits.
    1. Rabbits – Literary collection. [1. Rabbits – Literary collections.] I. Retan, Walter.
PZ5.B88 1991   90-41486
808.8'036 – dc20   CIP
                                                                                                    AC
ISBN 0-671-73220-X LSB, 0-671-73221-8

ACKNOWLEDGMENTS

Every effort has been made to trace the ownership of all copyrighted material and to secure the necessary permissions to reprint these selections. If any question arises as to the use of any material, the editor and the publisher, while expressing regret for any inadvertent error, will make the necessary correction in future printings.

Grateful acknowledgment is made to the following for permission to reprint copyrighted material:

Judith Ciardi for "The Easter Bunny" by John Ciardi. Crown Publishers, Inc. for LITTLE RABBIT'S LOOSE TOOTH by Lucy Bate, text copyright © 1975 by Lucy Bate, illustrations copyright © 1975 by Diane de Groat. Greenwillow Books (a div. of William Morrow & Co.) for HARRY'S SONG by Lillian Hoban, text and illustrations copyright © 1980 by Lillian Hoban. HarperCollins for US and Canadian rights for "Listen, Rabbit!" (Thomas Y. Crowell), copyright © 1964 by Aileen Fisher. Harrap Publishing Group Ltd. for "See the Little Bunny Sleeping" from MUSIC FOR THE NURSERY SCHOOL by Linda Chesterman. Robert Luce, Inc. for "Bunnies' Bedtime" and "Once I Saw a Bunny" from LET'S DO FINGERPLAYS by Marion Grayson. Macmillan Publishing Co. for US and Canadian rights to "The Story of the Blessing of El-ahrairah" from WATERSHIP DOWN by Richard Adams, copyright © 1972 by Richard Adams. McGraw-Hill, Inc. for "A Little Brown Rabbit" from GAMES FOR THE VERY YOUNG compiled by Elizabeth Matterson. Penguin UK for illustrations from THE TALE OF PETER RABBIT by Beatrix Potter, copyright 1902, © 1987 by Fredrick Warne & Co. Marion Reiner for "What in the World?" from THERE IS NO RHYME FOR SILVER by Eve Merriam, copyright © 1962 by Eve Merriam. Barbara K. Walker for HOW THE HARE TOLD THE TRUTH ABOUT HIS HORSE. Warner Chappell & Co. for PETER COTTONTAIL by Steve Nelson and Jack Rollins, copyright © 1950, renewed 1977 by Chappell & Co.; all rights reserved. Western Publishing Co., Inc. for "The Whispering Rabbit" from THE GOLDEN SLEEPY BOOK by Margaret Wise Brown, illustrated by Garth Williams, copyright © 1948, 1971 by Western Publishing, Co., Inc.

Illustrations on pages 10, 11, 18, 19, 40, 41, 54, and 55 by Heidi Petach.
Illustration on page 96 by Carolyn Ewing.

Contents

To the Reader

When I was a boy, one of my grandfathers had a farm not far from the town where I lived. Nothing was more fun than a trip to that farm. I could help my grandfather milk the cows, feed hay to the horses, or throw chicken feed to the hens. But the most fun was walking by myself through the fields, searching for wild rabbits. They seemed like little people the way they stood up on their hind legs, watching me intently with their bright eyes. I wanted so badly to pick one up, but they would let me get just *so* close. Then they hopped away, their long ears flapping in the breeze.

I spent a lot of time looking for rabbit holes. My grandfather had told me that rabbits always made at least two entrances to their tunnels so that they couldn't be trapped inside. When one of my friends was with me, we would hunt for the second entrance, then spend hours waiting—one of us at each entrance—for a bunny to come out. We never did see one. I'm sure we were making too much noise.

Eventually we discovered that there was a man in our town who sold tame rabbits. My mother wouldn't let me buy one, but two of my friends—brothers—bought a pair. We had a lot of fun feeding them lettuce and carrots and other vegetables. We also enjoyed holding them, patting their soft fur, and watching their little noses twitch as their bright, beady eyes examined us. However, I soon discovered why my mother hadn't wanted me to have a rabbit. Having grown up on a farm, she knew how fast they multiplied!

6

Soon my friends had more little bunnies than they could take care of. They had to start finding homes for them. That was not so much fun.

Rabbits are such appealing little creatures that it's no wonder they have been the subject of so many stories, poems, and songs. Aesop, the ancient Greek storyteller, wrote about them in fables such as ''The Tortoise and the Hare.'' The Brothers Grimm included them in fairy tales like ''The Hare and the Hedgehog.'' And it was a dignified White Rabbit, dressed in a waistcoat with a pocket watch, who led Alice down the rabbit hole into a wonderland full of amazing characters. There have even been stories about toy bunnies, like that perennial favorite, *The Velveteen Rabbit*.

In this collection you will find a rich sampling from the many wonderful poems, stories, and songs that have been written about rabbits. In addition to the titles mentioned above, there are works by such distinguished authors as Margaret Wise Brown, Lillian Hoban, John Ciardi, and Eve Merriam; and remarkable drawings by such famous illustrators as Beatrix Potter and Garth Williams. And as a special treat, the reader will discover songs and fingerplay rhymes involving—guess what?—BUNNIES, BUNNIES, BUNNIES!

What in the World?

What in the world
jumps with a hop and a bump
and a tail that can thump
has pink pointy ears and twitchy nose
looking for anything crunchy that grows?
A carroty lettucey cabbagey luncheon
To munch on?

Who knows?

Eve Merriam

Little Bunny Rabbits

Oh, little bunny rabbits,
  With funny little tails,
And ears so long you seem to me
  Like boats with furry sails,

You nibble at your cabbages;
  Your ears go flippy-flop.
Then all at once, you turn away,
  And hop and hop and hop!

Frances Arnold Greenwood

Hippity, Skippity, Hop

Hippity, Skippity, Hop
And away,
Little brown rabbits
Are busy today.

In the tall grasses,
See how they play.
Little brown rabbits
Are busy today.

Anonymous

See the Little Bunny Sleeping

See the little bunny sleeping,
Till it's nearly noon.
Come and let us gently wake him
With a merry tune.
Oh, how still!
Is he ill?
Wake up soon.

Hop, little bunny, hop, hop, hop.
Hop, little bunny, hop, hop, hop.

Anonymous

9

Once I Saw a Bunny

Once I saw a bunny
*Extend index and middle finger of
one hand upward.*

And a green, green,
cabbage head.
Make fist with other hand.

"I think I'll have some cabbage,"
The little bunny said.
So he nibbled and he nibbled,
*Make bobbing motion with ring finger
and thumb of first hand.*

And he pricked his ears to say,
*Extend index and middle fingers
upward.*

"Now I think it's time
I should be hopping on my way."
Let hand hop away.

Bunnies' Bedtime

"My bunnies now must go
to bed,"
Hold up hands; extend fingers.

"But I will count them first
to see
Point to fingers.

The little mother rabbit said.

If they have all come back
to me.

One bunny, two bunnies, three
bunnies dear,
Point to each finger as you count.

They are the prettiest
things alive—
My bunnies, one, two, three,
four, five."

Four bunnies, five bunnies—
yes, all are here.

Point to each finger again.
When counting out,
point to each child.

11

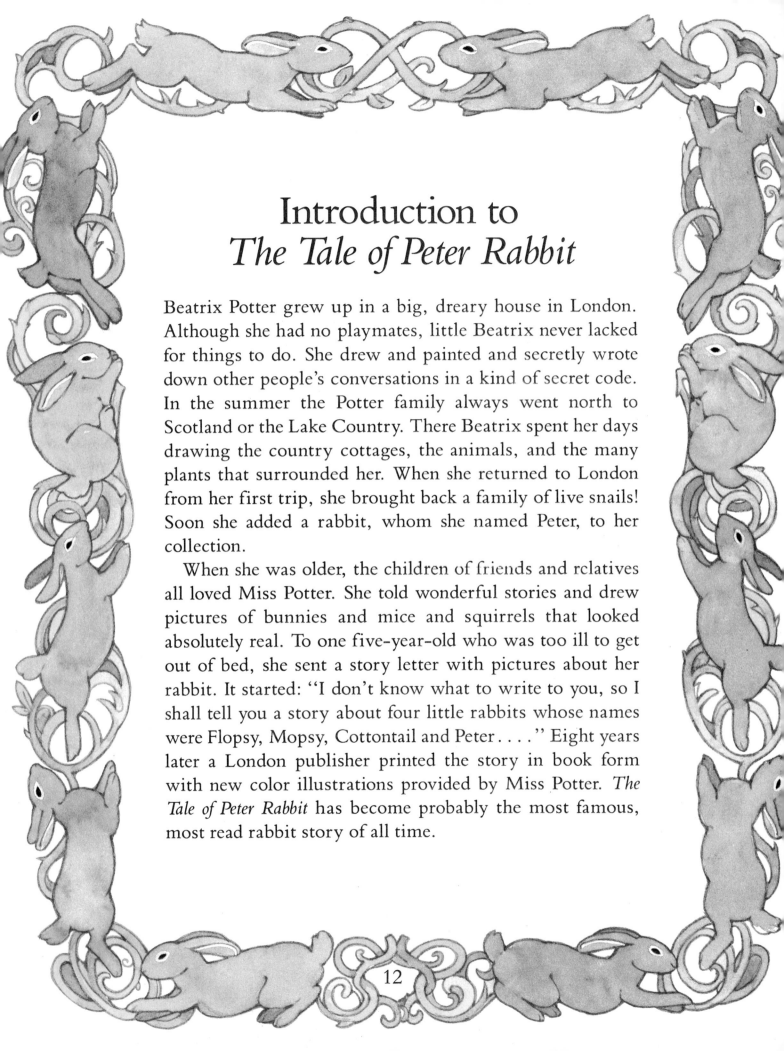

Introduction to
The Tale of Peter Rabbit

Beatrix Potter grew up in a big, dreary house in London. Although she had no playmates, little Beatrix never lacked for things to do. She drew and painted and secretly wrote down other people's conversations in a kind of secret code. In the summer the Potter family always went north to Scotland or the Lake Country. There Beatrix spent her days drawing the country cottages, the animals, and the many plants that surrounded her. When she returned to London from her first trip, she brought back a family of live snails! Soon she added a rabbit, whom she named Peter, to her collection.

When she was older, the children of friends and relatives all loved Miss Potter. She told wonderful stories and drew pictures of bunnies and mice and squirrels that looked absolutely real. To one five-year-old who was too ill to get out of bed, she sent a story letter with pictures about her rabbit. It started: "I don't know what to write to you, so I shall tell you a story about four little rabbits whose names were Flopsy, Mopsy, Cottontail and Peter...." Eight years later a London publisher printed the story in book form with new color illustrations provided by Miss Potter. *The Tale of Peter Rabbit* has become probably the most famous, most read rabbit story of all time.

The Tale of Peter Rabbit

story and pictures by Beatrix Potter

Once upon a time there were four little Rabbits, and their names were—Flopsy, Mopsy, Cotton-tail, and Peter.

They lived with their Mother in a sandbank, underneath the root of a very big fir tree.

"Now, my dears," said old Mrs. Rabbit one morning, "you may go into the fields or down the lane, but don't go into Mr. McGregor's garden: your Father had an accident there; he was put in a pie by Mrs. McGregor.

"Now run along, and don't get into mischief. I am going out."

Then old Mrs. Rabbit took a basket and her umbrella, and went through the wood to the baker's. She bought a loaf of brown bread and five currant buns.

Flopsy, Mopsy, and Cotton-tail, who were good little bunnies, went down the lane to gather blackberries; but Peter, who was very naughty, ran straightaway to Mr. McGregor's garden, and squeezed under the gate!

First he ate some lettuces and some French beans; and then he ate some radishes; and then, feeling rather sick, he went to look for some parsley.

But round the end of a cucumber frame, whom should he meet but Mr. McGregor!

Mr. McGregor was on his hands and knees planting out young cabbages, but he jumped up and ran after Peter, waving a rake and calling out, "Stop, thief!"

Peter was most dreadfully frightened; he rushed all over the garden, for he had forgotten the way back to the gate.

He lost one of his shoes among the cabbages, and the other shoe amongst the potatoes.

After losing them, he ran on four legs and went faster, so that I think he might have got away altogether if he had not unfortunately run into a gooseberry net, and got caught by the large buttons on his jacket. It was a blue jacket with brass buttons, quite new.

Peter gave himself up for lost, and shed big tears; but his sobs were overheard by some friendly sparrows, who flew to him in great excitement, and implored him to exert himself.

Mr. McGregor came up with a sieve, which he intended to pop upon the top of Peter; but Peter wriggled out just in time, leaving his jacket behind him.

And rushed into the toolshed, and jumped into a can. It would have been a beautiful thing to hide in, if it had not had so much water in it.

Mr. McGregor was quite sure that Peter was somewhere in the toolshed, perhaps hidden underneath a flowerpot. He began to turn them over carefully, looking under each.

Presently Peter sneezed—"Kertyschoo!" Mr. McGregor was after him in no time, and tried to put his foot upon Peter, who jumped out of a window, upsetting three plants. The window was too small for Mr. McGregor, and he was tired of running after Peter. He went back to his work.

Peter sat down to rest; he was out of breath and trembling with fright, and he had not the least idea which way to go. Also he was very damp with sitting in that can.

After a time he began to wander about, going lippity-lippity—not very fast, and looking all around.

He found a door in a wall; but it was locked, and there was no room for a fat little rabbit to squeeze underneath.

An old mouse was running in and out over the stone doorstep, carrying peas and beans to her family in the wood. Peter asked her the way to the gate, but she had such a large pea in her mouth that she could not answer. She only shook her head at him. Peter began to cry.

Then he tried to find his way straight across the garden, but he became more and more puzzled. Presently, he came to a pond where Mr. McGregor filled his water cans. A white cat was staring at some goldfish; she sat very, very still, but now and then the tip of her tail twitched as if it were alive. Peter thought it best to go away without speaking to her; he had heard about cats from his cousin, little Benjamin Bunny.

He went back towards the toolshed, but suddenly, quite close to him, he heard the noise of a hoe—sc-r-ritch, scratch, scratch, scritch. Peter scuttered underneath the bushes. But presently, as nothing happened, he came out, and climbed upon a wheelbarrow, and peeped over. The first thing he saw was Mr. McGregor hoeing onions. His back was turned towards Peter, and beyond him was the gate!

Peter got down very quietly off the wheelbarrow, and started running as fast as he could go, along a straight walk behind some black-currant bushes.

Mr. McGregor caught sight of him at the corner, but Peter did not care. He slipped underneath the gate, and was safe at last in the wood outside the garden.

Mr. McGregor hung up the little jacket and the shoes for a scarecrow to frighten the blackbirds.

Peter never stopped running or looked behind him till he got home to the big fir tree.

He was so tired that he flopped down upon the nice soft sand on the floor of the rabbit hole, and shut his eyes. His mother was busy cooking; she wondered what he had done with his clothes. It was the second little jacket and pair of shoes that Peter had lost in a fortnight!

I am sorry to say that Peter was not very well during the evening.

His mother put him to bed, and made some camomile tea; and she gave a dose of it to Peter!

"One tablespoonful to be taken at bedtime."

But Flopsy, Mopsy, and Cotton-tail had bread and milk and blackberries, for supper.

A Little Brown Rabbit

A little brown rabbit
popped out of the ground,
Right index finger pops up.

Wriggled his whiskers
and looked around.
Right index finger wriggles.

Another wee rabbit
who lived in the grass
Left index finger pops up.

Popped his head out
and watched him pass.
*Right hand hops over left
(wrists crossed).*

Then both the rabbits went
hoppity hop,
Hoppity, hoppity,
hoppity, hop,
Both index fingers hop forward.

Till they came to a wall
and had to stop.
Both fingers stop suddenly.

Then both the wee rabbits
turned themselves round,
Hands uncross.

And scuttled off home
to their holes in the ground.
*Hands hop back and finish
in pockets.*

The Tortoise and the Hare

a fable by Aesop
illustrations by Darcy May

Hare was making fun of Tortoise. "What a slowpoke you are!" he said. "I don't know how you get anywhere with those four short legs. Look at *my* long legs. And see how fast *I* can run."

Hare began to show off, hopping in circles around and around poor Tortoise.

Finally Tortoise had enough. "If you think you are so fast," he said, "why don't you race with me to the big rock on the top of Oak Hill?"

"Race with *you*!" Hare exclaimed. "What a silly fellow you are. You know very well that you can't beat me. But if it makes you happy, I'll be glad to race you to that rock. We'll soon find out who's faster."

After the other forest animals had gathered around to watch, Fox gave the signal for the race to begin.

Tortoise wasted no time. He started off at once, creeping slowly but steadily down the road. As for Hare, he leaped out of sight almost before you could say scat.

But it was no fun to race against someone he couldn't even see. After a while Hare stopped and sat down at the side of the road to wait for Tortoise. He would laugh at the slowpoke when he came plodding past.

The sun was very hot, and soon Hare began to feel drowsy. First one eye closed, then the other. Before he knew it he was fast asleep. He didn't even see Tortoise pass slowly down the road in the direction of the big rock.

"Slow and steady," Tortoise was muttering to himself. "That is the way to win a race."

After a long time, Hare woke up with a start. What was happening? Wasn't he supposed to be racing somebody?

Hare looked back down the road. Nobody there. He looked toward Oak Hill. What was that black speck crawling up the hill? Wasn't that Tortoise, getting very close to the big rock on Oak Hill!

Hare sprang up and started running as fast as he could go. But he was too late. By the time he reached the big rock, Tortoise was already there, waiting. Much ashamed, Hare crept away, leaving the other animals to congratulate the winner.

"Just as I always say," Tortoise repeated, "slow and steady wins the race."

Harry's Song

story and pictures by Lillian Hoban

The long fall shadow crept over the hill. It covered the rock where Harry Rabbit sat quietly singing. It chilled his toes and cooled his nose.

"Hurry, Harry," called his mother, Mrs. Rabbit. "It is getting late."

Harry didn't move.

"One hot, hot golden summer day," sang Harry softly. *"The good green smell of sweet warm grass."*

24

"That's a lovely song, Harry," said Mrs. Fieldmouse as she hurried past. "Come along, children," she called. Five fat little Fieldmouse children came up the hill pulling a large basket of fall seeds.

"What are you singing?" they asked.

"*The hazy, lazy rich ripe taste of August,*" sang Harry. "*Bees buzzing in the honey-heavy air.*"

"That's a summertime song, Harry," cried the little Fieldmouse children. "It's fall now."

They pushed the basket into the hole where Mrs. Fieldmouse stood waiting.

"That Harry is such a dreamer," said Mrs. Fieldmouse to her husband. "He hasn't even started to get ready for winter."

"Harry is a dumb bunny," said Mr. Fieldmouse. "He doesn't know enough to come in out of the cold." And Mr. Fieldmouse stored all the seeds his children had brought home in a large bin.

The fall shadow crept higher over the hill. But Harry did not move. A cold wind ruffled his fur. It blew in his ears and stirred his whiskers.

"Hurry home, Harry," called his mother from the burrow below. "It is getting very late."

Harry sat very still, singing softly.

"Red roses in the garden, black-eyed susans on the hill."

"No time to be singing, Harry," said old Mr. Chipmunk as he came hurrying past. Mr. Chipmunk's cheeks were stuffed with seeds. He had seeds in his pockets and seeds in his paws and a sack full of wheatgrass on his back.

"Time to get ready for winter," puffed Mr. Chipmunk. "Time to store food for the cold days ahead."

"Rows of leafy lettuces just rabbit-high and tender," sang Harry. *"Plump pods of sweet peas climbing on the vine."*

"Now, Harry, said Mr. Chipmunk, "that's a very nice song, but you really should think of your folks. They need more than a song to carry them through the winter."

Harry didn't move. He sat there in the wind and the cold of the late fall evening and sang:

"And in daisy-deep meadows a song-bird trills and under the fern a young rabbit sits still."

"Well," said Mr. Chipmunk, "you sure are a funny little bunny, Harry. It's a good thing all your brothers are hard-working rabbits or you and your family would go hungry all winter." Old Mr. Chipmunk shook his head and hurried off.

The long fall shadow darkened into night. A thin new moon shone softly on the rock where Harry sat.

"Harry," called Mrs. Rabbit. "Do come home. It is very late."

Harry didn't move. He sat very still. Deep deep inside, so no one could hear, he sang his song.

A little brown bat came flitting by. He swooped low over Harry and cried, "Winter is coming! Winter is coming! Time to fatten up for the long cold ahead."

27

Harry didn't move.

The little brown bat darted and dipped in the dark of the night. "Harry," cried the little brown bat, "bring home some grain, bring home some greens, or you and your folks will grow thin thin thin in the cold and the snow of winter!"

Harry sat very still with his eyes closed. Deep deep inside so no one could hear he remembered summer and sang his song.

The little brown bat scooped up a moth and headed for home. "Harry," he called, "won't you bring home some bark, won't you bring home some twigs? Won't you bring your folks a little SOMETHING?"

Harry was very quiet. He just sat in the wind and the cold and silently sang his summertime song.

"Oh, you are a bothersome bumbling bunny!" cried the little brown bat.

And he flew into his hollow tree to hole up for the winter.

"Harry," called Mrs. Rabbit, "where are you, Harry? Your brothers are all here. We miss you, Harry. Please come home."

Harry opened his eyes and jumped off the rock and hopped down the hill and straight into the den where his mother and brothers were waiting.

One of his brothers was sorting some grain.

And one of his brothers was sorting some greens.

One of his brothers was storing some bark, and one of his brothers was storing some twigs.

"Here's Harry!" they cried, "and he hasn't brought anything home for winter."

"Yes I have," said Harry. And he sang his song.

"Oh, Harry," said his mother, "how lovely! You've brought home the song of a perfect summer day to carry us through the winter. You are a honey of a bunny!"

And she hugged him very hard.

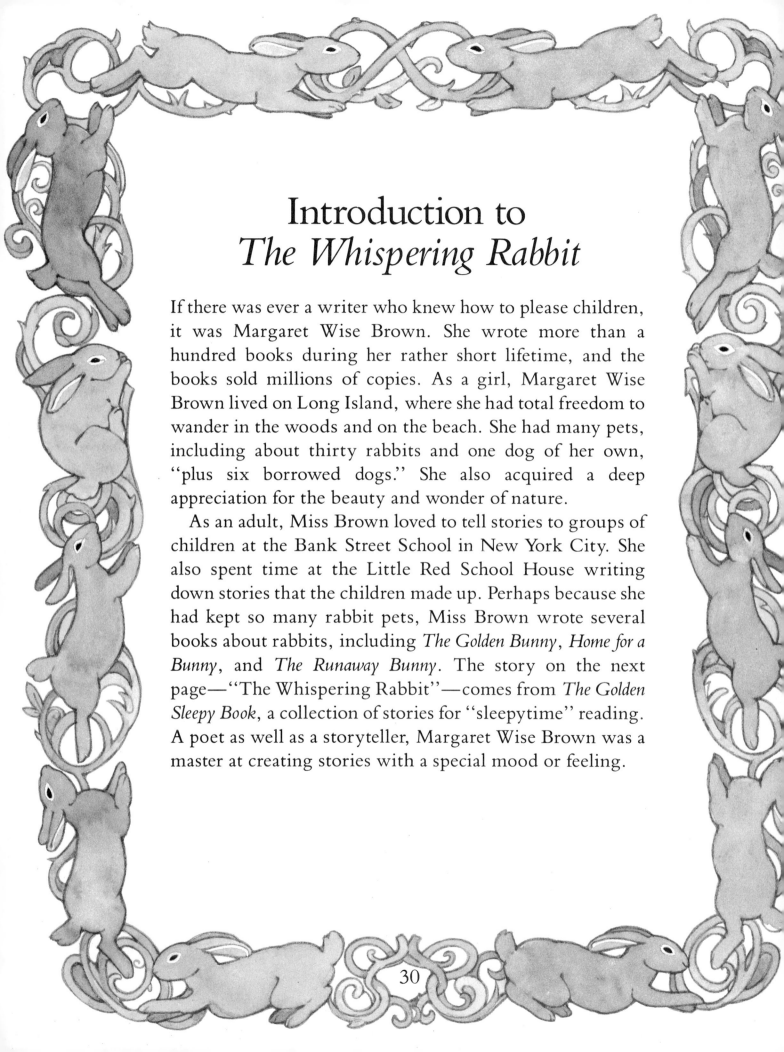

Introduction to
The Whispering Rabbit

If there was ever a writer who knew how to please children, it was Margaret Wise Brown. She wrote more than a hundred books during her rather short lifetime, and the books sold millions of copies. As a girl, Margaret Wise Brown lived on Long Island, where she had total freedom to wander in the woods and on the beach. She had many pets, including about thirty rabbits and one dog of her own, "plus six borrowed dogs." She also acquired a deep appreciation for the beauty and wonder of nature.

As an adult, Miss Brown loved to tell stories to groups of children at the Bank Street School in New York City. She also spent time at the Little Red School House writing down stories that the children made up. Perhaps because she had kept so many rabbit pets, Miss Brown wrote several books about rabbits, including *The Golden Bunny*, *Home for a Bunny*, and *The Runaway Bunny*. The story on the next page—"The Whispering Rabbit"—comes from *The Golden Sleepy Book*, a collection of stories for "sleepytime" reading. A poet as well as a storyteller, Margaret Wise Brown was a master at creating stories with a special mood or feeling.

The Whispering Rabbit

from THE GOLDEN SLEEPY BOOK

by Margaret Wise Brown
pictures by Garth Williams

Once there was a sleepy little rabbit
Who began to yawn—
And he yawned and he yawned and he yawned and
he yawned,
"Hmmm—"
He opened his little rabbit mouth when he yawned till
you could see his white front teeth and his little round pink
mouth, and he yawned and he yawned until suddenly a bee
flew into his mouth and he swallowed the bee.

31

"Hooo— hooo—," said a fat old owl. "Always keep your paw in front of your mouth when you yawn," hooted the owl.

"Rabbits never do that," said the sleepy little rabbit.

"Silly rabbits!" said the owl and he flew away.

The little rabbit was just calling after him, but when the little rabbit opened his mouth to speak the bumblebee had curled up to sleep in his throat—AND—all he could do was whisper.

"What shall I do?" he whispered to a squirrel who wasn't sleepy.

"Wake him up," said the squirrel. "Wake up the bumblebee."

"How?" whispered the rabbit. "All I can do is whisper and I'm sleepy and I want to go to sleep and who can sleep with a bumblebee—"

Suddenly a wise old groundhog popped up out of the ground.

"All I can do is whisper," said the little rabbit.

"All the better," said the groundhog.

"Come here, little rabbit," he said, "and I will whisper to you how to wake up a bumblebee.

"You have to make the littlest noise that you can possibly make because a bumblebee doesn't bother about big noises. He is a very little bee and he is only interested in little noises."

"Like a loud whisper?" asked the rabbit.

"Too loud," said the groundhog and popped back into his hole.

"A little noise," whispered the rabbit and he started making little rabbit noises—he made a noise as quiet as the sound of a bird's wing cutting the air, but the bee didn't wake up. So the little rabbit made the sound of snow falling but the bee didn't wake up.

So the little rabbit made the sound of a bug breathing and a fly sneezing and grass rustling and a fireman thinking. Still the bee didn't wake up. So the rabbit sat and thought of all the little sounds he could think of—What could they be?

A sound quiet as snow melting, quiet as a flower growing, quiet as an egg, quiet as— And suddenly he knew the little noise that he would make—and he made it.

It was like a little click made hundreds of miles away by a bumblebee in an apple tree in full bloom on a mountain top. It was the very small click of a bee swallowing some honey from an apple blossom.

34

And at that the bee woke up.

He thought he was missing something and away he flew.

And then what did the little rabbit do? That sleepy sleepy little rabbit?

He closed his mouth
He closed his eyes
He closed his ears
And he tucked in his paws
And twitched his nose
And he went sound asleep!

The Very First Easter Rabbit

traditional tale and rebus
illustrations by Roberta Collier

Once there was a long, dark time when winter came and would not leave. At

first the  enjoyed making and fighting snowball battles,

but after weeks and weeks of this they began to long for spring. Spring was

their favorite time of year, but it seemed that it might never come again.

So the  went to the woods to look for spring. On the first day they

looked high and low for their friends the , but there was not a

 to be found. Nothing but . Sadly, the trudged

home to their suppers.

The next day the went back to the woods. They searched

for a sign of a , but there were no anywhere. Nothing

but . Cold and shivering, the went home.

The next day the went out looking for a . But there

was not a to be found, not even a . Once again, the children

trudged home through the .

Day after day the children went to the woods. If only spring would

come! They looked for  on the , and and

 , and and . But the would not melt,

and the would not shine. At last the were so discouraged

that they gave up going to the woods altogether. They simply stayed in their

homes and slept.

But then, as if by magic, the did come out. The melted,

the rivers swelled, and the and began to bloom. Best

of all, the woodland creatures awoke from their winter sleeps and came out of

their dens. And while all these wonderful things happened, there were no

in the woods to enjoy them, for all the were dozing by the fire

at home.

The stretched his hind legs and said, "Spring has come at last!

But where are the ? It isn't spring without !"

"Spring was very late this year," said the . "Perhaps the

thought it wasn't coming."

"Then we must let them know that spring is here!" said the .

"Why don't you go into town and tell them, ?"

"I would like to," said the . "But I must finish building my

. Maybe will go."

"I would like to," said the . "But the  are afraid of me.

Maybe  will go."

"I would like to," said the . "But the townspeople will chase me

away. Maybe will go."

"I would like to," said the , who was sitting timidly under a tree.

"But I am much too shy to talk to ."

"Then go at night when they are sleeping," said the .

The missed the very much, so he agreed to go. The other

animals helped him prepare. The  gathered grass and twigs, which

the wove into tiny . The filled the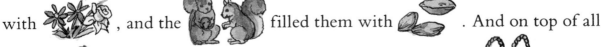

with 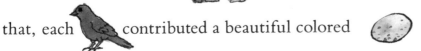, and the filled them with . And on top of all

that, each 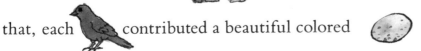 contributed a beautiful colored . The were so full of spring treasures that their meaning was clear: Spring was here at last.

When night fell and the were sleeping, the hopped

quietly into town. At each child's , he left a lovely spring .

He hopped back into the woods before dawn.

The next morning was warm and sunny. And what a surprise met the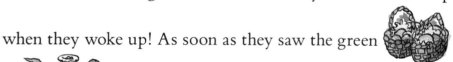

when they woke up! As soon as they saw the green full of

and and , they knew that winter was over at last. They

followed the 's tracks into the woods, and there they found the

 gone, the and  in bloom, and all the animals

waiting to greet them. They played in the warm  all day long.

And that's how  have celebrated spring ever since.

Listen, Rabbit!

"Listen, rabbit!"
I laughed and cried,
feeling all shiny
and warm inside.
"What a wonderful
secret surprise I've spied,
what a wonderful secret
for you to hide."

I hadn't a pony
or pup
to pet,

I hadn't a rabbit
exactly, yet,

But I
had a nest
like a fur-lined cup

And *five baby rabbits*
to watch grow up!

Aileen Fisher

40

The Easter Bunny

There once was an egg that felt funny.
It was chocolate brown, and got runny
    When a clucky old hen
    Sat to hatch it, and when
She was done, what popped out was—a bunny!

Said the hen, looking down, "Well, I say!
You're a strange looking chick! But please stay
    Till you learn to say *peep*."
    "There's a date I must keep,"
Said the bunny, and hip-hopped away.

He did say, "Mrs. Hen, I thank you.
But I'm hatched now, and have work to do.
    Besides, it is best
    I get out of this nest,
For it's covered with chocolate goo."

He left then. And where did he go?
The fact is I really don't know.
    He might have come here
    Look around you, my dear.
What's that on your bed?—Well, hello!

John Ciardi

41

The Hare and the Hedgehog

a fairy tale by the Brothers Grimm
illustrations by Christopher Santoro

Once upon a time there was a very clever hedgehog. This hedgehog was a gentleman farmer, and he grew the finest corn in the country. One morning as he walked through his green field, the hedgehog came upon his neighbor, the hare.

"Good morning, sir," said the hedgehog. "Would you like to join me on my walk?"

The hare only grunted and replied, "It's a wonder you *can* walk on such stubby little legs." He said this because he envied the hedgehog's fine corn so very much.

Now, the hedgehog was normally a good-natured fellow, but he took offense at insults just like anyone else. So he decided to teach his neighbor a lesson.

"My legs may be stubby," he said in as dignified a manner as he could muster, "but even so I am sure I can run faster than you can."

"One sack of gold says you can't," replied the hare.

"As you wish," said the hedgehog. "But before we race, I must have my breakfast. Meet me back here in one hour, and the contest will begin."

The hare agreed and hopped speedily away, while the hedgehog slowly lumbered home. Once there he called for his wife and explained to her what had happened.

"Oh, dear!" cried the hedgehog's wife. "What shall we do? You are sure to lose that race, and a sack of gold with it!"

"Never fear, my dear," said the hedgehog. "I have a plan."

And a splendid plan it was. The hedgehog dressed his
wife to look exactly as he himself looked, from his hat down
to his boots. Then he led her to the cornfield and told her
what to do.

"Hare and I will race from one end of the cornfield to the
other," he explained. "You shall stand at the end of this row
of corn and pretend to be me. Then it will look as if I had won
the race!"

The hedgehog's wife approved of the plan. She scurried
to the end of her row of corn and hid.

Before long the hare arrived, carrying a sack of gold. "I hope you have brought one, too," he said haughtily, "for you are bound to lose it."

"We shall see what we shall see," the clever hedgehog said mysteriously.

The hare and the hedgehog each stood at the end of a row of corn. Then, "Go!" shouted the hedgehog, and away the hare sprinted. But when he reached the other end of the cornfield, there stood the hedgehog's wife.

The hare could not believe his eyes. "There must be some mistake," he said.

"There is no mistake," said the hedgehog's wife. "Why don't we race again?"

So the hare bounded through the field, only to meet the hedgehog himself on the other side.

"How can it be?" said the hare in disbelief.

"Perhaps you are not as quick as you think," said the hedgehog.

Over and over again, the hare ran through the field. And every time, there was a hedgehog at the end of it, laughing at him.

At last the hare gave up. He gave the hedgehog his sack of gold without so much as a whimper.

That night the hedgehog and his wife celebrated their victory. And it was not long before everyone in the countryside heard about the race between the hare and the hedgehog. Many years passed before anyone dared to tease the hedgehog about his short legs again.

Little Rabbit's Loose Tooth

by Lucy Bate
pictures by Diane de Groat

Little Rabbit had a loose tooth. It was her first loose tooth, and it wiggled a lot. At suppertime Little Rabbit said, "You know I cannot eat carrots and beans. I have a loose tooth."

But Father Rabbit said, "Carrots and beans are very good for little rabbits."

"They are too hard," said Little Rabbit, "for little rabbits with a loose tooth."

"Oh?" said Mother Rabbit. "And what is soft enough for a little rabbit with a loose tooth?"

Little Rabbit thought for a while. There were strawberries in the refrigerator. "Strawberries," she said, "soft strawberries."

"You can have strawberries for dessert," said Mother Rabbit. "And you can chew the carrots and beans with your other teeth."

"Are you sure?" said Little Rabbit.

"I'm sure," said Mother Rabbit.

"Are you sure, Daddy?" asked Little Rabbit.

"I'm sure," said Father Rabbit. "I've done it myself."

That was on Monday.

On Tuesday Little Rabbit chewed oranges with her loose tooth and cucumbers with her other teeth.

On Wednesday she chewed watermelon with her loose tooth and lettuce with her other teeth.

On Thursday she chewed vanilla pudding with her loose tooth and cabbage with her other teeth.

On Friday she chewed spinach with her other teeth and chocolate ice cream with her loose tooth, and the loose tooth came right out in the chocolate ice cream.

"I have a tooth in my chocolate ice cream," said Little Rabbit.

"That's wonderful," said Mother Rabbit.

"It's about time," said Father Rabbit.

"What should I do with it?" asked Little Rabbit.

"You should take it out of your chocolate ice cream," answered Mother Rabbit.

Little Rabbit took the tooth out of the chocolate ice cream. "I have a window in my mouth," she said. "I can stick my tongue through it."

"That's amazing," said Mother Rabbit.

Little Rabbit put some chocolate ice cream in the window in her mouth.

"Look," she said. "I have a chocolate tooth in my mouth."

"How tasty!" said Father Rabbit.

Little Rabbit finished her dish of ice cream. Then she licked the chocolate ice cream off the tooth and took it to the sink and put the plug in the sink. She gave it a bath in cold water. Then she dried it with the dishtowel and took it back to the table.

"What should I do with my tooth?" she asked.

"Whatever you want," said Mother Rabbit.

"I could throw it away," said Little Rabbit.

"Or, you could put it under your pillow for the tooth fairy," said Mother Rabbit.

"Why should I do that?" asked Little Rabbit.

"When you are asleep the tooth fairy will take your tooth and leave you a present," said Mother Rabbit.

"Does the tooth fairy get to keep my tooth?"

"Yes, of course," said Mother Rabbit.

Little Rabbit put her tongue in the window in her mouth. Then she took her tongue out of the window. "What if I don't want the tooth fairy to keep my tooth?" she said.

"Then there's no point in putting your tooth under your pillow," said Mother Rabbit.

"I don't believe in the tooth fairy, anyway," said Little Rabbit.

"No?" said Mother Rabbit.

"No," said Little Rabbit. "There are lots of things you can do with a tooth besides give it to a tooth fairy."

Little Rabbit took her tooth and went into her room and thought about the things she could do.

She could make a hole in it and put a string through it and wear it for a necklace.

But then she thought the tooth might break when she tried to make the hole.

She could paste it on a piece of paper and draw stars around it and hang it on her bedroom wall.

But then she thought that might look silly.

She could put it in her pocket and take it to the candy store and try to buy some candy with it.

But then she thought maybe the rabbit who owned the candy store would say that a tooth is not a penny.

Then Little Rabbit thought she could throw the tooth away, but she did not really want to do that, either.

Little Rabbit went into the living room where Mother Rabbit was playing the flute.

"Mommy," she said, "what if I believe in the tooth fairy?"

Mother Rabbit put down her flute. "Then you'd better put your tooth under your pillow before you lose it. You can put it in an envelope if you want."

Little Rabbit found an envelope and put the tooth in it. Then she went into her room and put the envelope under her pillow. Little Rabbit came back to the living room.

"What kind of presents do tooth fairies leave?" she asked.

"Well," said Mother Rabbit, "what do you think?"

"I think they leave whatever they want," said Little Rabbit. "Money?"

"Not a lot of money," said Mother Rabbit.

Little Rabbit thought for a minute. "A penny?"

"Well, maybe a dime."

"A dime is smaller than a penny," Little Rabbit said.

"It's smaller but it's worth more," said Mother Rabbit. "A dime is worth ten pennies."

"I know that," Little Rabbit said. "I just wanted to make sure."

"Daddy," said Little Rabbit, "I believe in the tooth fairy."

Father Rabbit put down his newspaper so Little Rabbit could climb up into his lap. "And what do you think the tooth fairy wants with your tooth?"

"She wants to give me money," said Little Rabbit.

"Oh, I see," said Father Rabbit. "And what will she do with your tooth after she gives you money?"

"I think she will save my tooth and give it to a baby rabbit that was just born, and that's how little baby rabbits get teeth. Do you think that, Daddy?"

"Ah—" said Father Rabbit.

"Or," said Little Rabbit, "I think she will put my tooth up in the sky because it is such a shiny tooth, and that's how stars get made. Do you think that, Daddy?"

"We-l-l," said Father Rabbit.

"Really," said Little Rabbit, "I think she says a magic spell and she turns the tooth into a penny, I mean a dime. Do you think that, Daddy?"

"I think," said Father Rabbit, "that it is your bedtime."

"Okay, but would you please remind Mommy about my believing in the tooth fairy in case she forgets."

"I could," said Father Rabbit.

"My tooth is in an envelope under my pillow."

"That's good," said Father Rabbit.

"I have a window in my mouth."

"Window or no window," said Father Rabbit, "it is time for bed." He gave her a good-night kiss. "Good night, Little Rabbit."

"Good night, Daddy."

Little Rabbit got into her pajamas and brushed her teeth and turned off the light and got into bed.

Mother Rabbit came to kiss her good night.

"Mommy," said Little Rabbit.

"Yes?" said Mother Rabbit.

"Just in case there isn't a tooth fairy," said Little Rabbit.

"Yes?" said Mother Rabbit.

"After I'm asleep, could you sneak and look under my pillow and look in the envelope? And if there isn't a present, could *you* leave one?"

"Yes," said Mother Rabbit.

"You don't have to tell me," said Little Rabbit. "You could just sneak."

"All right," said Mother Rabbit. "Now good night, Little Rabbit."

"Good night, Mommy," said Little Rabbit, and she went to sleep.

The stars came out. And the moon rose up in the east. And the moon set in the west. And the stars went in. The sun came up. It was morning.

Little Rabbit woke up. She looked under her pillow. She took out the envelope. She opened it.

And inside the envelope was a dime.

The Rabbit

When they said the time to hide was mine,
I hid back under a thick grape vine.

And while I was still for the time to pass,
A little gray thing came out of the grass.

He hopped his way through the melon bed
And sat down close by a cabbage head.

He sat down close where I could see,
And his big still eyes looked hard at me,

His big eyes bursting out of the rim,
And I looked back very hard at him.

Elizabeth Madox Roberts

The Toad
and the Rabbit

Said the Rabbit to the Hop Toad:
   "It's very strange to me
How very big and long and wide
   A Hop Toad's *mouth* can be."

Said the Hop Toad to the Rabbit:
   "I'm sure I'd shed some tears
If on my head I had to wear
   Such flippy-floppy ears."

John Martin

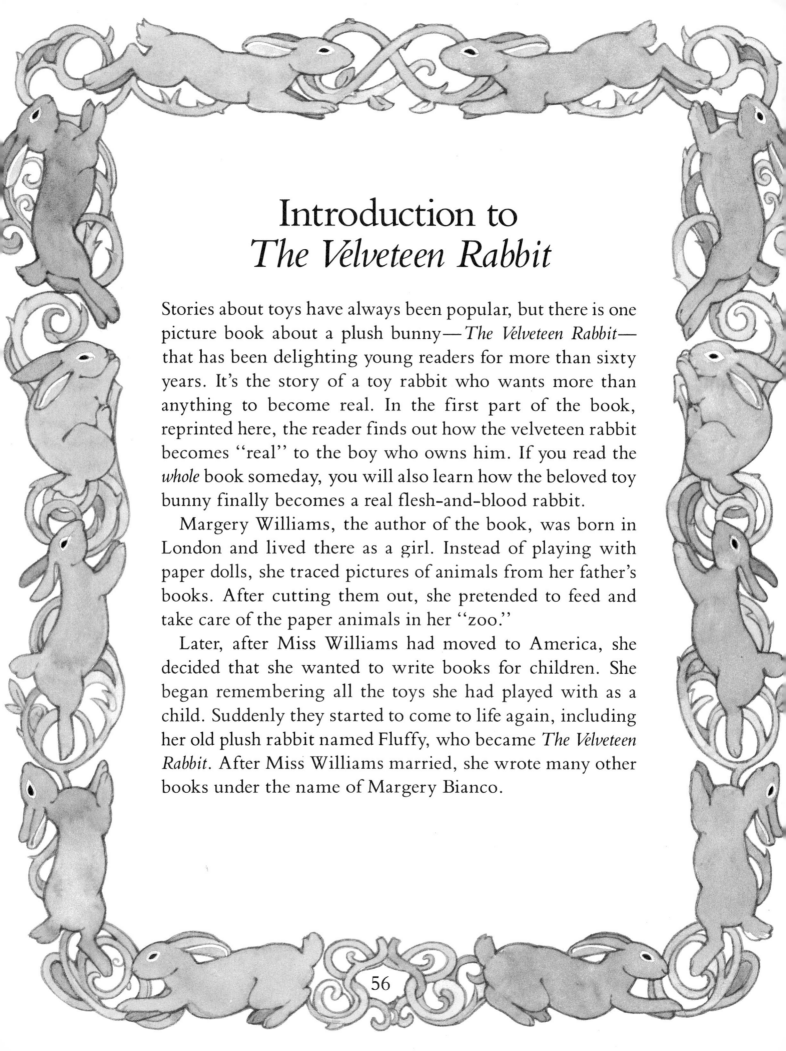

Introduction to
The Velveteen Rabbit

Stories about toys have always been popular, but there is one picture book about a plush bunny—*The Velveteen Rabbit*—that has been delighting young readers for more than sixty years. It's the story of a toy rabbit who wants more than anything to become real. In the first part of the book, reprinted here, the reader finds out how the velveteen rabbit becomes "real" to the boy who owns him. If you read the *whole* book someday, you will also learn how the beloved toy bunny finally becomes a real flesh-and-blood rabbit.

Margery Williams, the author of the book, was born in London and lived there as a girl. Instead of playing with paper dolls, she traced pictures of animals from her father's books. After cutting them out, she pretended to feed and take care of the paper animals in her "zoo."

Later, after Miss Williams had moved to America, she decided that she wanted to write books for children. She began remembering all the toys she had played with as a child. Suddenly they started to come to life again, including her old plush rabbit named Fluffy, who became *The Velveteen Rabbit*. After Miss Williams married, she wrote many other books under the name of Margery Bianco.

from
The Velveteen Rabbit
or How Toys Become Real
by Margery Williams

illustrations by Natalie Carabetta

There was once a velveteen rabbit, and in the beginning he was really splendid. He was fat and bunchy, as a rabbit should be; his coat was spotted brown and white, he had real thread whiskers, and his ears were lined with pink sateen. On Christmas morning, when he sat wedged in the top of the Boy's stocking, with a sprig of holly between his paws, the effect was charming.

There were other things in the stocking, nuts and oranges and a toy engine, and chocolate almonds and a clockwork mouse, but the Rabbit was quite the best of all. For at least two hours the Boy loved him, and then Aunts and Uncles came to dinner, and there was a great rustling of tissue paper and unwrapping of parcels, and in the excitement of looking at all the new presents the Velveteen Rabbit was forgotten.

For a long time he lived in the toy cupboard or on the nursery floor, and no one thought very much about him. He was naturally shy, and since he was only made of velveteen, some of the more expensive toys quite snubbed him. The mechanical toys were very superior, and looked down upon everyone else; they were full of modern ideas, and pretended they were real. The model boat, who had lived through two seasons and lost most of his paint, caught the tone from them and never missed an opportunity of referring to his rigging in technical terms. The Rabbit could not claim to be a model of anything, for he didn't know that real rabbits existed; he thought they were all stuffed with sawdust like himself, and he understood that sawdust was quite out-of-date and should never be mentioned in modern circles. Even Timothy, the jointed wooden lion, who was made by the disabled soldiers, and should have had broader views, put on airs and pretended he was connected with Government. Between them all the poor little Rabbit was made to feel himself very insignificant and commonplace, and the only person who was kind to him at all was the Skin Horse.

The Skin Horse had lived longer in the nursery than any of the others. He was so old that his brown coat was bald in patches and showed the seams underneath, and most of the hairs in his tail had been pulled out to string bead necklaces. He was wise, for he had seen a long succession of mechanical toys arrive to boast and swagger, and by-and-by break their mainsprings and pass away, and he knew that they were only toys, and would never turn into anything else. For nursery magic is very strange and wonderful, and only those playthings that are old and wise and experienced like the Skin Horse understand all about it.

"What is REAL?" asked the Rabbit one day, when they were lying side by side near the nursery fender, before Nana came to tidy the room. "Does it mean having things that buzz inside you and a stick-out handle?"

"Real isn't how you are made," said the Skin Horse. "It's a thing that happens to you. When a child loves you for a long, long time, not just to play with, but REALLY loves you, then you become Real."

"Does it hurt?" asked the Rabbit.

"Sometimes," said the Skin Horse, for he was always truthful. "When you are Real you don't mind being hurt."

"Does it happen all at once, like being wound up," he asked, "or bit by bit?"

"It doesn't happen all at once," said the Skin Horse. "You become. It takes a long time. That's why it doesn't often happen to people who break easily, or have sharp edges, or who have to be carefully kept. Generally, by the time you are Real, most of your hair has been loved off, and your eyes drop out and you get loose in the joints and very shabby. But these things don't matter at all, because once you are Real you can't be ugly, except to people who don't understand."

"I suppose *you* are Real?" said the Rabbit. And then he wished he had not said it, for he thought the Skin Horse might be sensitive. But the Skin Horse only smiled.

"The Boy's Uncle made me Real," he said. "That was a great many years ago; but once you are Real you can't become unreal again. It lasts for always."

The Rabbit sighed. He thought it would be a long time before this magic called Real happened to him. He longed to become Real, to know what it felt like; and yet the idea of growing shabby and losing his eyes and whiskers was rather sad. He wished that he could become it without these uncomfortable things happening to him.

There was a person called Nana who ruled the nursery. Sometimes she took no notice of the playthings lying about, and sometimes, for no reason whatever, she went swooping about like a great wind and hustled them away in cupboards. She called this "tidying up," and the playthings all hated it, especially the tin ones. The Rabbit didn't mind it so much, for wherever he was thrown he came down soft.

One evening, when the Boy was going to bed, he couldn't find the china dog that always slept with him. Nana was in a hurry, and it was too much trouble to hunt for china dogs at bedtime, so she simply looked about her, and seeing that the toy cupboard door stood open, she made a swoop.

"Here," she said, "take your old Bunny! He'll do to sleep with you!" And she dragged the Rabbit out by one ear, and put him into the Boy's arms.

That night, and for many nights after, the Velveteen Rabbit slept in the Boy's bed. At first he found it rather uncomfortable, for the Boy hugged him very tight, and sometimes he rolled over on him, and sometimes he pushed him so far under the pillow that the Rabbit could scarcely breathe. And he missed, too, those long moonlight hours in the nursery, when all the house was silent, and his talks with the Skin Horse. But very soon he grew to like it, for the Boy used to talk to him, and made nice tunnels for him under the bedclothes that he said were like the burrows the real rabbits lived in. And they had splendid games together, in whispers, when Nana had gone away to her supper and left the night-light burning on the mantelpiece. And when the Boy dropped off to sleep, the Rabbit would snuggle down close under his little warm chin and dream, with the Boy's hands clasped close round him all night long.

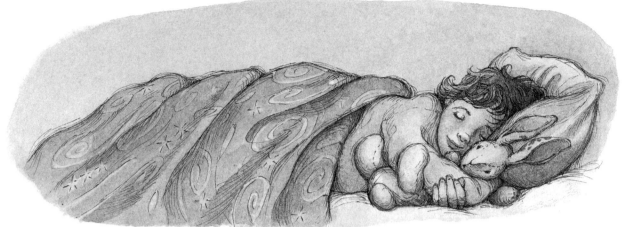

And so time went on, and the little Rabbit was very happy—so happy that he never noticed how his beautiful velveteen fur was getting shabbier and shabbier, and his tail coming unsewn, and all the pink rubbed off his nose where the Boy had kissed him.

Spring came, and they had long days in the garden, for wherever the Boy went the Rabbit went too. He had rides in the wheelbarrow, and picnics on the grass, and lovely fairy huts built for him under the raspberry canes behind the flower border. And once, when the Boy was called away

suddenly to go out to tea, the Rabbit was left out on the lawn until long after dusk, and Nana had to come and look for him with the candle because the Boy couldn't go to sleep unless he was there. He was wet through with the dew and quite earthy from diving into the burrows the Boy had made for him in the flower bed, and Nana grumbled as she rubbed him off with a corner of her apron.

"You must have your old Bunny!" she said. "Fancy all that fuss for a toy!"

The Boy sat up in bed and stretched out his hands.

"Give me my Bunny!" he said. "You mustn't say that. He isn't a toy. He's REAL!"

When the little Rabbit heard that he was happy, for he knew that what the Skin Horse had said was true at last. The nursery magic had happened to him, and he was a toy no longer. He was Real. The Boy himself had said it.

That night he was almost too happy to sleep, and so much love stirred in his little sawdust heart that it almost burst.

How the Hare Told the Truth About His Horse

an East African legend
retold by Barbara K. Walker
illustrations by Roberta Collier

Once long ago a man and a lion were good friends,
just like brothers.

Day after day, the lion came to visit the man.
Every day the lion said, "Some day, when we are truly best
friends, I want you to come to visit me."

Now, the hare had watched the man and the lion. He,
too, wanted to be the man's friend. What could he do to make
the man want him as his friend, perhaps even as his brother?

"I know!" he said one day. "I must prove that I am the master of the lion. But that is not easily done."

He thought and thought again. Finally he smiled. He had a good plan. Now he must try it.

He went to the man. "I would like to have you as my brother," he said.

The man laughed. "Thank you, but I already have a brother. The lion is my brother."

"The lion?" the hare laughed. "The lion is nobody. Didn't you know? The lion is no more than my horse."

"Your horse?" said the man. "I cannot believe that."

The hare went home. That afternoon, the lion came to see the man. Suddenly the man began to laugh. "So you are the hare's horse!" he said.

"Who told you I was the hare's horse?" asked the lion, surprised.

"The hare himself told me," said the man. "I cannot believe it. All the same, it may be true. After all, the hare said it was true."

The lion lashed his tail in anger. "I shall find the hare and teach him to speak the truth," he said.

He looked here and there and everywhere.

At last he found the hare. "So you told the man I was your horse!" he said crossly. "It is a lie. You know I am not your horse."

"Of course you are not my horse," said the hare, laughing at such a foolish idea. "The man misunderstood. If I did not feel so ill, I would go and tell him myself. But, alas, I am not well enough to walk."

"Very well," said the lion, "I will carry you there. Then you can tell the man the truth."

The lion crouched down. Carefully the hare climbed onto his back.

"Are you ready?" asked the lion.

"I am ready," said the hare.

The lion began to walk toward the man's village. The hare swayed from side to side as the lion walked.

66

"Wait!" called the hare. "I am becoming very dizzy. I cannot go to tell the man after all."

The lion stopped. "You MUST tell the man," he said. "He will not be my brother if he thinks I am no better than the hare's horse. What can I do to make you ride more comfortably?"

The hare thought for a minute. "Perhaps we could make a bridle from that grapevine over there," he said. "We could put the bridle in your mouth, and that would give me something to hold on to."

"All right," said the lion, and they made a fine bridle from the grapevine. It was passed through the lion's mouth. The lion crouched down again. Once more, the hare climbed on his back. The lion began walking again toward the man's village.

Slap! Slap! The hare began slapping at the flies around him. "Wait!" he called. "I cannot go to tell the man after all. These flies are making me very dizzy."

The lion stopped. "You MUST tell the man," he said. "I do not wish to have him believe such an untruth. What can we do to drive away the flies?"

"If I had a small whip to hold," said the hare, "I believe I could drive them away. See. There is a bush by the path. We could take a small branch from that."

The lion broke off a small branch as a whip. Carefully the hare trimmed off all the leaves. "Now!" he said. "That should do. Now I can manage nicely, I think."

The lion crouched down. Once more, the hare climbed on his back. He held the ends of the bridle in one front paw and the whip in the other. Carefully the lion began to walk. Tug-tug went the bridle. Slap-slap went the whip. Yes, the hare managed very nicely.

At last they came to the man's house. He was sitting outside. When he saw them coming, he began to laugh.

"You will not laugh when you hear the truth spoken by the hare," said the lion with great dignity. "Tell him, hare."

"O man," said the hare, sitting proudly on the back of the lion, "you can see for yourself whether or not the lion is my horse. The judgment of your eyes is more sound than anything either I or the lion could say."

Too late, the lion recognized the truth: that he had indeed become the hare's horse. As for the hare, he was well satisfied. And the man? He has laughed each time the story has been told down the long years till now.

Why Rabbit Has a Short Tail

a fable by Aesop
illustrations by John O'Brien

One sunny day, Rabbit decided to take a walk through the forest. He went up and down hills, and climbed over big rocks.

Rabbit soon came to the Great Swamp. This swamp was the home of Hungry Old Alligator. But Rabbit wasn't afraid. He was sure he was much smarter and faster than Alligator.

Now Rabbit was beginning to feel tired, and he didn't want to walk all the way around the Great Swamp. He looked around and saw Alligator basking in the warm sun. Alligator could carry me across, he thought. But Alligator would try to *eat* me, too! So Rabbit had to think of something clever.

"Hello there, Hungry Old Alligator!" called Rabbit. "You sure must be lonely! I heard you scared away everyone in your family."

"Nonsense! There are thousands in my family, and they all live right here in this swamp!" said Alligator.

"I'll have to count them to believe you," said Rabbit.

So Alligator called his whole family over, and they all piled together.

"I can't count you all like this!" Rabbit cried. "You must line up in a straight line across the swamp."

So all the alligators lined up, one behind the other, across the Great Swamp. Hungry Old Alligator (who was also quite clever) put himself at the end of the line. He sat quietly and waited.

Rabbit stepped onto the back of the first alligator and started counting "One, two, three . . ." as he quickly hopped across the swamp. When he reached the end of the line, Hungry Old Alligator fiercely snapped at him. But Rabbit jumped clear and continued hopping across the countryside.

Finally, Rabbit stopped to dust himself off. How clever I am, Rabbit thought. But then he tried to dust off his tail— and it was just about gone! Alligator had bitten off a good part of it, and all that remained was a stubby little puffball.

And that is why rabbits have such small tails today.

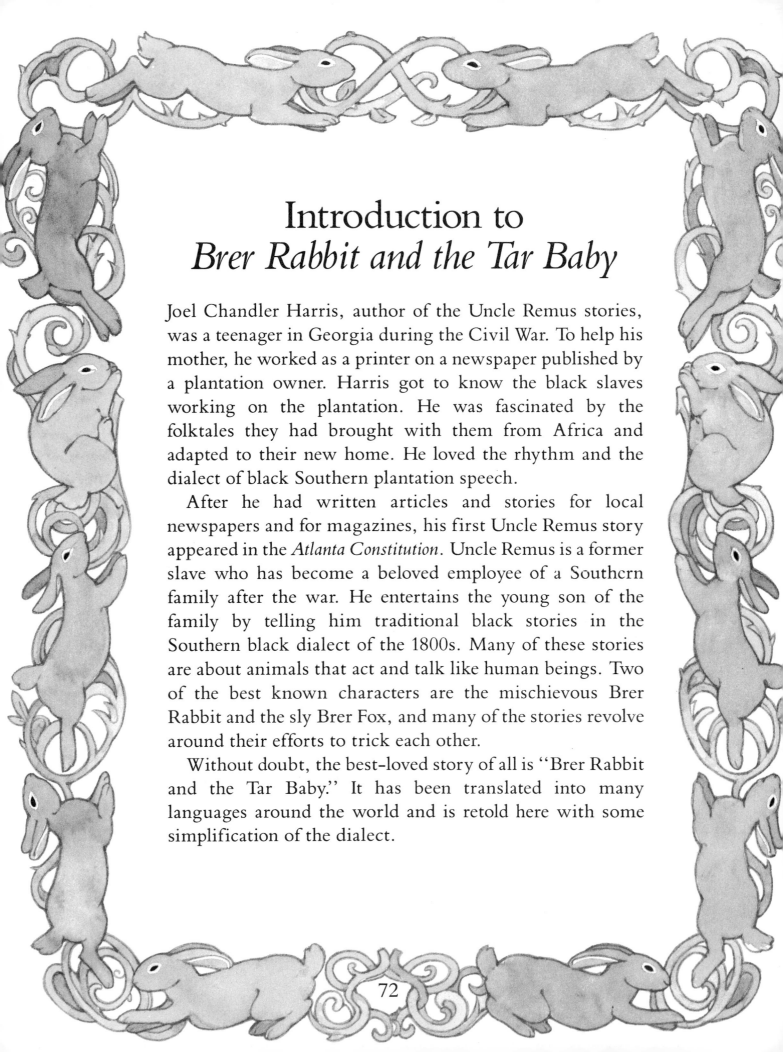

Introduction to
Brer Rabbit and the Tar Baby

Joel Chandler Harris, author of the Uncle Remus stories, was a teenager in Georgia during the Civil War. To help his mother, he worked as a printer on a newspaper published by a plantation owner. Harris got to know the black slaves working on the plantation. He was fascinated by the folktales they had brought with them from Africa and adapted to their new home. He loved the rhythm and the dialect of black Southern plantation speech.

After he had written articles and stories for local newspapers and for magazines, his first Uncle Remus story appeared in the *Atlanta Constitution*. Uncle Remus is a former slave who has become a beloved employee of a Southern family after the war. He entertains the young son of the family by telling him traditional black stories in the Southern black dialect of the 1800s. Many of these stories are about animals that act and talk like human beings. Two of the best known characters are the mischievous Brer Rabbit and the sly Brer Fox, and many of the stories revolve around their efforts to trick each other.

Without doubt, the best-loved story of all is "Brer Rabbit and the Tar Baby." It has been translated into many languages around the world and is retold here with some simplification of the dialect.

Brer Rabbit and the Tar Baby

Afro-American folktale retold by Walter Retan
illustrations by John O'Brien

One day, after Brer Rabbit had tricked him so many times, Brer Fox got himself some sticky tar and mixed it with some turpentine and fixed up a contraption that he called a Tar Baby. He took the Tar Baby and set it down right smack in the big road. Then he lay down in the bushes and watched to see what was goin' to happen.

Brer Fox didn't have to wait long either. By and by Brer Rabbit came prancin' down the road—*lippity-clippity, clippity-lippity*—just as sassy as a jay bird. Brer Fox he lay low. Brer Rabbit came prancin' right along till he spied the Tar Baby settin' there.

"Mornin'!" says Brer Rabbit. "How is your health this mornin'?"

Brer Fox, he wink his eye slow. Tar Baby—he ain't sayin' nothin'.

"How come you're not answerin' me?" asks Brer Rabbit. "Is you deaf? Because if you is, I can holler louder."

Tar Baby just kept on settin' there, and Brer Fox he still layin' low.

"You're mighty stuck up," says Brer Rabbit. "But I'm goin' to cure you—that's what I'm goin' to do," he says.

Brer Fox sort-a chuckle in his stomach, but Tar Baby ain't sayin' nothin'.

"If you don't take off that old hat and say howdy-do to me," says Brer Rabbit, "I'm goin' to bust you wide open."

Tar Baby stay still, and Brer Fox—he lay low.

Brer Rabbit kept on askin' Tar Baby to say howdy-do and Tar Baby kept on sayin' nothin' at all till finally Brer Rabbit drew back his fist and—*blip!*—he hit Tar Baby right smack on the side of his head.

But that was a big mistake. His fist stuck to Tar Baby fast and tight.

"If you don't let me loose, I'll knock you again," says Brer Rabbit, and he fetched Tar Baby a swipe with the other hand. And *that* stuck too.

"Turn me loose," hollers Brer Rabbit, "before I kick the stuffin' out of you." But Tar Baby just keeps holdin' fast, so Brer Rabbit starts to kick. Before he knows it both his feet are stuck fast. Now Brer Rabbit yells out that if Tar Baby doesn't turn him loose, he'll butt him with his head.

Sure enough, Brer Rabbit butts and gets his head stuck too.

At that, Brer Fox came walkin' out of the bushes, lookin' just as innocent as a mockin' bird.

"Howdy, Brer Rabbit," says Brer Fox. "You look sort-a stuck up this mornin'." And he rolled over on the ground and laughed and laughed till he couldn't laugh no more. "I reckon

75

you're goin' to have dinner with me this time, Brer Rabbit," he says. "I been lookin' forward to some fine barbecued rabbit."

Brer Rabbit knew for sure that he was in real trouble now. He began to talk mighty humble.

"I don't care what you do with me, Brer Fox," he says, "just so you don't throw me in that brier patch."

"I declare," says Brer Fox, "it's so much trouble to build a fire that I may just have to hang you instead."

"Hang me as high as you please, Brer Fox," says Brer Rabbit, "but *please*—I beg of you—don't throw me in that brier patch."

"I just remembered," says Brer Fox, "I ain't got no string so I figure I'll just have to drown you."

"Drown me just as deep as you please, Brer Fox," says Brer Rabbit. "Anything! Just so long as you don't throw me in that brier patch."

Brer Fox wanted to punish Brer Rabbit just as bad as he could, so he caught him up by his hind legs and slung him right in the middle of the brier patch. There was a considerable crash where Brer Rabbit landed in the bushes, and Brer Fox hung around to see what was goin' to happen.

By and by he hear somebody call him. Away up on the hill Brer Rabbit sat cross-legged on a log, combin' the tar out of his hair. Poor Brer Fox knew he had been tricked once more.

As for Brer Rabbit—he just *had* to shout out one more piece of sass. "I was bred and born in a brier patch, Brer Fox, bred and born in a brier patch," he shouted as he skipped on up the hill out of sight.

Peter Cottontail

Moderately

Words and Music by Steve Nelson and Jack Rollins

Here comes Pe - ter Cot - ton - tail, Hop - pin' down the bun - ny trail,
Hip - pi - ty hop - pin', Eas - ter's on its way. _____
Look at him stop and lis - ten to him say: _____

Bring - in' ev - 'ry girl and boy Bas - kets full of Eas - ter joy,
"Try to do the things you should." May - be if you're ex - tra good,

Things to make your Eas - ter bright and gay. _____ He's got
He'll roll lots of Eas - ter eggs your way. _____ You'll wake

jel - ly beans for Tom - my, Col - ored eggs for sis - ter Sue. There's an
up on Eas - ter morn - ing, And you'll know that he was there When you

or - chid for your mom - my And an Eas - ter bon - net, too. ·Oh!
find those choc - 'late bun - nies that he's hid - ing ev - 'ry - where. Oh!

here comes Pe - ter Cot - ton - tail, Hop - pin' down the bun - ny trail,

1.
Hip - pi - ty hop - pi - ty, Hap - py Eas - ter Day.

2.
Day. _____

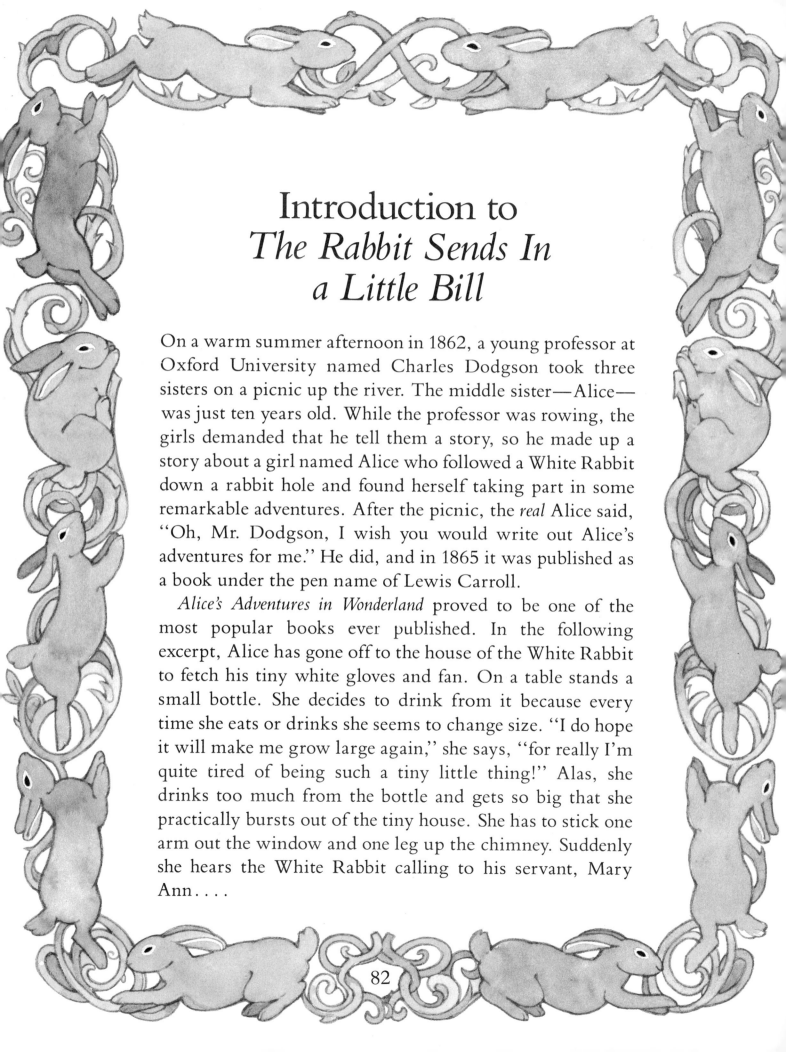

Introduction to
The Rabbit Sends In a Little Bill

On a warm summer afternoon in 1862, a young professor at Oxford University named Charles Dodgson took three sisters on a picnic up the river. The middle sister—Alice—was just ten years old. While the professor was rowing, the girls demanded that he tell them a story, so he made up a story about a girl named Alice who followed a White Rabbit down a rabbit hole and found herself taking part in some remarkable adventures. After the picnic, the *real* Alice said, "Oh, Mr. Dodgson, I wish you would write out Alice's adventures for me." He did, and in 1865 it was published as a book under the pen name of Lewis Carroll.

Alice's Adventures in Wonderland proved to be one of the most popular books ever published. In the following excerpt, Alice has gone off to the house of the White Rabbit to fetch his tiny white gloves and fan. On a table stands a small bottle. She decides to drink from it because every time she eats or drinks she seems to change size. "I do hope it will make me grow large again," she says, "for really I'm quite tired of being such a tiny little thing!" Alas, she drinks too much from the bottle and gets so big that she practically bursts out of the tiny house. She has to stick one arm out the window and one leg up the chimney. Suddenly she hears the White Rabbit calling to his servant, Mary Ann....

from
The Rabbit Sends In a Little Bill

from the classic Alice's Adventures in Wonderland
by Lewis Carroll
with the original illustrations by Sir John Tenniel

"Mary Ann! Mary Ann!" said the voice. "Fetch me my gloves this moment!" Then came a little pattering of feet on the stairs. Alice knew it was the Rabbit coming to look for her, and she trembled till she shook the house, quite forgetting that she was now about a thousand times as large as the Rabbit, and had no reason to be afraid of it.

Presently the Rabbit came up to the door, and tried to open it; but, as the door opened inwards, and Alice's elbow was pressed hard against it, that attempt proved a failure. Alice heard it say to itself, "Then I'll go round and get in at the window."

"*That* you won't!" thought Alice, and after waiting till she fancied she heard the Rabbit just under the window, she suddenly spread out her hand, and made a snatch in the air. She did not get hold of anything, but she heard a little shriek and a fall, and a crash of broken glass, from which she concluded that it was just possible it had fallen into a cucumber-frame, or something of the sort.

Next came an angry voice—the Rabbit's—"Pat! Pat! Where are you?" And then a voice she had never heard before, "Sure then I'm here! Digging for apples, yer honour!"

"Digging for apples, indeed!" said the Rabbit angrily. "Here! Come help me out of *this*!" (Sounds of more broken glass.)

"Now tell me, Pat, what's that in the window?"

"Sure, it's an arm, yer honour!" (He pronounced it "arrum.")

"An arm, you goose! Who ever saw one that size? Why, it fills the whole window!"

"Sure, it does, yer honour: but it's an arm for all that."

"Well, it's got no business there, at any rate: go and take it away!"

There was a long silence after this, and Alice could only hear whispers now and then; such as "Sure, I don't like it, yer honour, at all, at all!" "Do as I tell you, you coward!" and at last she spread out her hand again, and made another snatch in the air. This time there were *two* little shrieks, and more sounds of broken glass. "What a number of cucumber-frames there must be!" thought Alice. "I wonder what they'll do next! As for pulling me out of the window, I only wish *they could*! I'm sure *I* don't want to stay in here any longer!"

She waited for some time without hearing anything more: at last came a rumbling of little cart-wheels, and the sound of a good many voices all talking together: she made out the words: "Where's the other ladder?—Why, I hadn't to bring but one. Bill's got the other—Bill! Fetch it here, lad!—Here, put 'em up at this corner—No, tie 'em together first—they don't reach half high enough yet—Oh, they'll do well enough. Don't be particular—Here, Bill! Catch hold of this rope—Will the roof bear?—Mind that loose slate—Oh, it's coming down! Heads below!" (a loud crash)—"Now, who did that?—It was Bill, I fancy—Who's to go down the chimney?—Nay *I* shan't! *You* do it! *That* I won't then!—Bill's got to go down—Here, Bill! The master says you've got to go down the chimney!"

"Oh, so Bill's got to come down the chimney, has he?" said Alice to herself. "Why, they seem to put everything upon Bill! I wouldn't be in Bill's place for a good deal: this fireplace is narrow, to be sure; but I *think* I can kick a little!"

She drew her foot as far down the chimney as she could, and waited till she heard a little animal (she couldn't guess of

what sort it was) scratching and scrambling about in the chimney close above her: then, saying to herself "This is Bill," she gave one sharp kick, and waited to see what would happen next.

The first thing she heard was a general chorus of "There goes Bill!" then the Rabbit's voice alone—"Catch him, you by the hedge!" then silence, and then another confusion of voices—"Hold up his head—Brandy now—Don't choke him—How was it, old fellow? What happened to you? Tell us all about it!"

Last came a little feeble, squeaking voice ("That's Bill," thought Alice), "Well I hardly know—No more, thank ye; I'm better now—but I'm a deal too flustered to tell you—all I know is, something comes at me like a Jack-in-the-box, and up I goes like a sky-rocket!"

"So you did, old fellow!" said the others.

"We must burn the house down!" said the Rabbit's voice. And Alice called out, as loud as she could, "If you do, I'll set Dinah at you!"

There was a dead silence instantly, and Alice thought to herself "I wonder what they *will* do next! If they had any sense, they'd take the roof off." After a minute or two they began moving about again, and Alice heard the Rabbit say "A barrowful will do, to begin with."

"A barrowful of *what*?" thought Alice. But she had not long to doubt, for the next moment a shower of little pebbles came rattling in at the window, and some of them hit her in the face. "I'll put a stop to this," she said to herself, and shouted out, "You'd better not do that again!" which produced another dead silence.

Alice noticed, with some surprise, that the pebbles were all turning into little cakes as they lay on the floor, and a bright idea came into her head. "If I eat one of these cakes," she thought, "it's sure to make *some* change in my size; and, as it can't possibly make me larger, it must make me smaller, I suppose."

So she swallowed one of the cakes, and was delighted to find that she began shrinking directly. As soon as she was small enough to get through the door, she ran out of the house, and found quite a crowd of little animals and birds waiting outside. The poor little Lizard, Bill, was in the middle, being held up by two guinea-pigs, who were giving it something out of a bottle. They all made a rush at Alice the moment she appeared; but she ran off as hard as she could, and soon found herself safe in a thick wood.

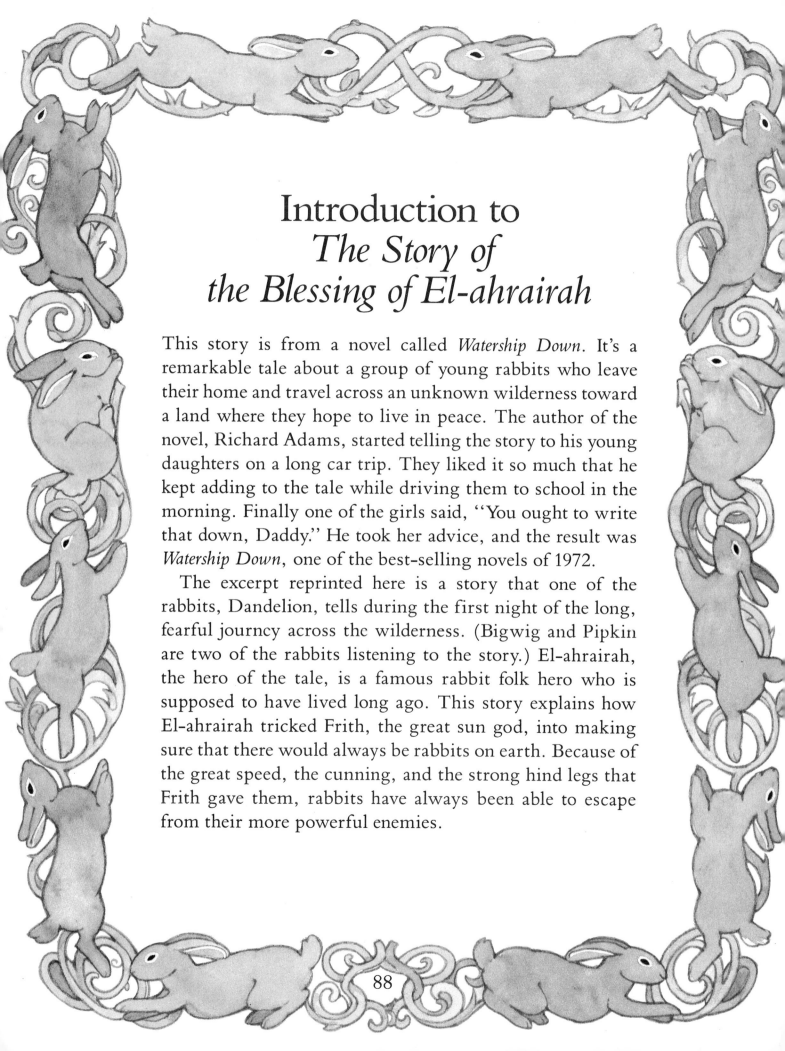

Introduction to
The Story of the Blessing of El-ahrairah

This story is from a novel called *Watership Down*. It's a remarkable tale about a group of young rabbits who leave their home and travel across an unknown wilderness toward a land where they hope to live in peace. The author of the novel, Richard Adams, started telling the story to his young daughters on a long car trip. They liked it so much that he kept adding to the tale while driving them to school in the morning. Finally one of the girls said, ''You ought to write that down, Daddy.'' He took her advice, and the result was *Watership Down*, one of the best-selling novels of 1972.

The excerpt reprinted here is a story that one of the rabbits, Dandelion, tells during the first night of the long, fearful journey across the wilderness. (Bigwig and Pipkin are two of the rabbits listening to the story.) El-ahrairah, the hero of the tale, is a famous rabbit folk hero who is supposed to have lived long ago. This story explains how El-ahrairah tricked Frith, the great sun god, into making sure that there would always be rabbits on earth. Because of the great speed, the cunning, and the strong hind legs that Frith gave them, rabbits have always been able to escape from their more powerful enemies.

The Story of the Blessing of El-ahrairah

from WATERSHIP DOWN

by Richard Adams
illustrations by Natalie Carabetta

"Long ago, Frith made the world. He made all the stars, too, and the world is one of the stars. He made them by scattering his droppings over the sky and this is why the grass and the trees grow so thick on the world. Frith makes the rivers flow. They follow him as he goes through the sky, and when he leaves the sky they look for him all night. Frith made all the animals and birds, but when he first made them they were all the same. The sparrow and the kestrel were friends and they both ate seeds and flies. And the fox and the rabbit were friends and they both ate grass. And there was plenty of grass and plenty of flies, because the world was new and Frith shone down bright and warm all day.

"Now, El-ahrairah was among the animals in those days and he had many wives. He had so many wives that there was no counting them, and the wives had so many young that even Frith could not count them, and they ate the grass and the dandelions and the lettuces and the clover, and El-ahrairah was the father of them all." (Bigwig growled appreciatively.) "And after a time," went on Dandelion, "after a time the grass began to grow thin and the rabbits wandered everywhere, multiplying and eating as they went.

"Then Frith said to El-ahrairah, 'Prince Rabbit, if you cannot control your people, I shall find ways to control them. So mark what I say.' But El-ahrairah would not listen and he said to Frith, 'My people are the strongest in the world, for they breed faster and eat more than any of the other people. And this shows how much they love Lord Frith, for of all the animals they are the most responsive to his warmth and brightness. You must realize, my lord, how important they are and not hinder them in their beautiful lives.'

"Frith could have killed El-ahrairah at once, but he had a mind to keep him in the world, because he needed him to

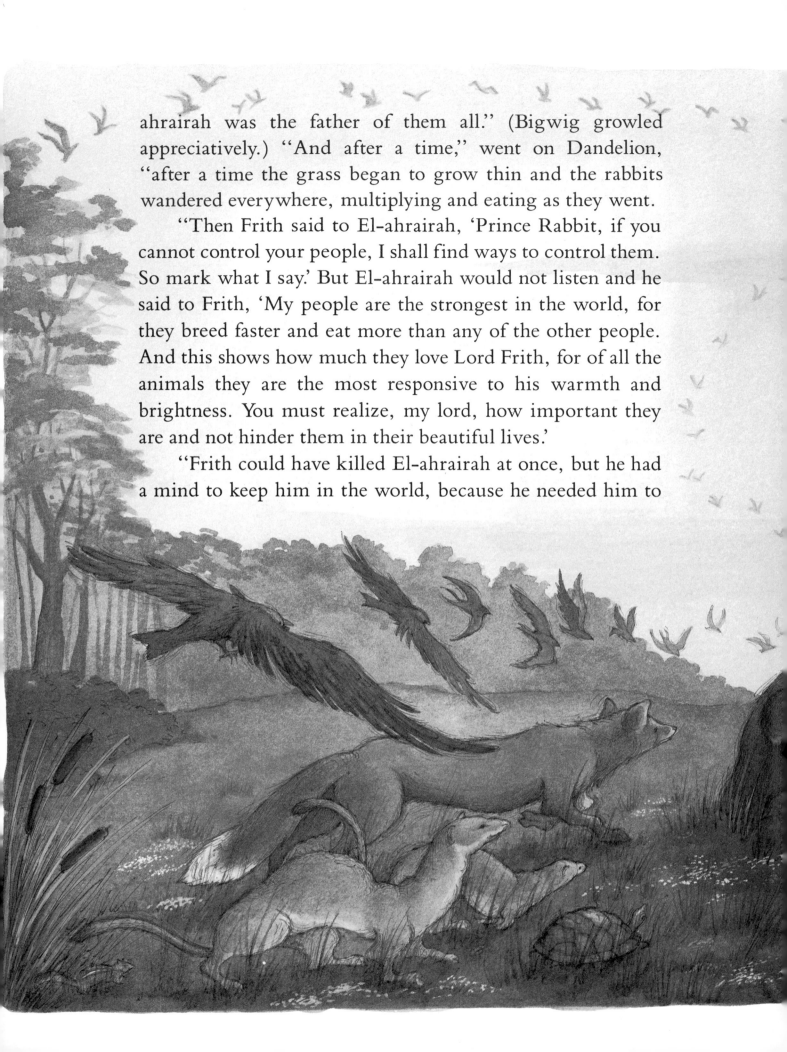

sport and jest and play tricks. So he determined to get the better of him, not by means of his own great power but by means of a trick. He gave out that he would hold a great meeting and that at that meeting he would give a present to every animal and bird, to make each one different from the rest. And all the creatures set out to go to the meeting place. But they all arrived at different times, because Frith made sure that it would happen so. And when the blackbird came, he gave him his beautiful song, and when the cow came, he gave her sharp horns and the strength to be afraid of no other creature. And so in their turn came the fox and the stoat and the weasel. And to each of them Frith gave the cunning and the fierceness and the desire to hunt and slay and eat the children of El-ahrairah. And so they went away from Frith full of nothing but hunger to kill the rabbits.

"Now, all this time El-ahrairah was dancing and mating and boasting that he was going to Frith's meeting to receive a great gift. And at last he set out for the meeting place. But as he was going there, he stopped to rest on a soft, sandy hillside. And while he was resting, over the hill came flying the dark swift, screaming as he went, 'News! News! News!' For you know, this is what he has said ever since that day. So El-ahrairah called up to him and said, 'What news?' 'Why,' said the swift, 'I would not be you, El-ahrairah. For Frith has given the fox and the weasel cunning hearts and sharp teeth, and to the cat he has given silent feet and eyes that can see in the dark, and they are gone away from Frith's place to kill and devour all that belongs to El-ahrairah.' And he dashed on over the hills. And at that moment El-ahrairah heard the voice of Frith calling, 'Where is El-ahrairah? For all the others have taken their gifts and gone and I have come to look for him.'

"Then El-ahrairah knew that Frith was too clever for him and he was frightened. He thought that the fox and the weasel were coming with Frith and he turned to the face of the hill and began to dig. He dug a hole, but he had dug only a little of it when Frith came over the hill alone. And he saw El-ahrairah's bottom sticking out of the hole and the sand flying out in showers as the digging went on. When he saw that, he called out, 'My friend, have you seen El-ahrairah, for I am looking for him to give him my gift?' 'No,' answered El-ahrairah, without coming out, 'I have not seen him. He is far away. He could not come.' So Frith said, 'Then come out of that hole and I will bless you instead of him.' 'No, I cannot,' said El-ahrairah, 'I am busy. The fox and the weasel are coming. If you want to bless me you can bless my bottom, for it is sticking out of the hole.'"

All the rabbits had heard the story before: on winter nights, when the cold draft moved down the warren passages and the icy wet lay in the pits of the runs below their burrows; and on summer evenings, in the grass under the red may and the sweet, carrion-scented elder bloom. Dandelion was telling it well, and even Pipkin forgot his weariness and danger and remembered instead the great indestructibility of the rabbits. Each one of them saw himself as El-ahrairah, who could be impudent to Frith and get away with it.

"Then," said Dandelion, "Frith felt himself in friendship with El-ahrairah, who would not give up even when he thought the fox and the weasel were coming. And he said, 'Very well, I will bless your bottom as it sticks out of the hole. Bottom, be strength and warning and speed forever and save the life of your master. Be it so!' And as he spoke, El-ahrairah's tail grew shining white and flashed like a star:

and his back legs grew long and powerful and he thumped the hillside until the very beetles fell off the grass stems. He came out of the hole and tore across the hill faster than any creature in the world. And Frith called after him, 'El-ahrairah, your people cannot rule the world, for I will not have it so. All the world will be your enemy, Prince with a Thousand Enemies, and whenever they catch you, they will kill you. But first they must catch you, digger, listener, runner, prince with the swift warning. Be cunning and full of tricks and your people shall never be destroyed.' And El-ahrairah knew then that although he would not be mocked, yet Frith was his friend. And every evening, when Frith has done his day's work and lies calm and easy in the red sky, El-ahrairah and his children and his children's children come out of their holes and feed and play in his sight, for they are his friends and he has promised them that they can never be destroyed.''

The Bunnies All
Sleep Soundly

The bunnies all sleep soundly,
Beneath the moon's bright ray;
They nod their heads together,
And dream the night away.

Anonymous